Mum and Dad.

Mum, Kipper and Dad.

Mum, Kipper, Dad and Chip.

Biff, Mum, Kipper, Dad, Chip,

and Floppy.

Printed in Hong Kong

SEA TO SHINING SEA

by Walker Hughes
Illustrated by Art Ruiz (pencil & ink)
Carlo Lo Raso (colorist)

SCHOLASTIC INC.

New York   Toronto   London   Auckland   Sydney
Mexico City   New Delhi   Hong Kong   Buenos Aires

ISBN 0-439-45187-6
HASBRO and its logo, G.I. JOE and all related characters are trademarks
of Hasbro, and are used with permission.
© 2003 Hasbro.
All Rights Reserved. Published by Scholastic Inc.
SCHOLASTIC and associated logos are trademarks and/or registered trademarks of Scholastic Inc.

12 11 10 9 8 7 6 5 4 3 2 1   3 4 5 6 7 8/0

Printed in the U.S.A.
First printing, March 2003

It was the dead of night. At the G.I. JOE headquarters, Duke heard the alarm first.

EMERGENCY!
TOP SECRET!
The computer screen flashed.
STEALTH PLANE DOWN!
PLANE CRASH!

The American stealth plane had crashed into the ocean. It was now stuck on the ocean floor. Luckily, the pilot escaped.

It was up to the G.I. JOE team to bring the top secret stealth plane home — before anyone else found it!

"Wet-Suit! Snake Eyes!" Duke called out. "Get ready for a deep-sea mission!"

The sun rose, peeking through dark storm clouds. Shipwreck piloted the powerboat over the waves. Wet-Suit and Snake Eyes scanned the ocean for any sign of COBRA.

Their mission was to dive for the plane, fix it, and fly it out again.

"Good luck," said Shinwreck.

Whup-whup-whup-whup-whup!
The noise of a helicopter broke the morning quiet.
"It's a COBRA copter!" said Wet-Suit.
"A Dominator!"

"Get to that plane before the COBRA
agents do!" Shipwreck ordered.
Lightning lit the sky. A storm was coming.
"Better hurry," said Shipwreck.

Snake Eyes nodded. He could only talk in sign language. But actions often speak louder than words.

Snake Eyes gave the signal. He and
Wet-Suit flipped backward into the ocean.
They dove deep into the icy water.

They swam down, fast as rockets.
If they could fix the plane's magnetic
field, it would be invisible. COBRA
would not see it.

Splash! Two COBRA agents dropped into the water. It was Storm Shadow and Moray!

"Shark Strike!" Moray shouted. His voice was loud and clear over his special underwater speakers.

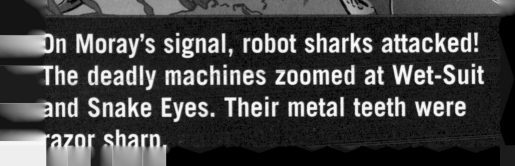

On Moray's signal, robot sharks attacked! The deadly machines zoomed at Wet-Suit and Snake Eyes. Their metal teeth were razor sharp.

The robot sharks circled...
closer...and closer...
Snake Eyes and Wet-Suit had to
escape — but how?

In a flash, Snake Eyes and Wet-Suit dove deeper — right to the ocean floor. They swam into a narrow cave.

Wet-Suit found an old fishing net. He grabbed it. "This must have drifted in here years ago!" Wet-Suit said. "Let's use it!"

Snake Eyes took the other end of the net. He and Wet-Suit swam out of the cave — right toward the robot sharks! They tumbled over, and under, and around and around.

"We got them!" said Wet-Suit. "Now let's get rid of these minnows!"
On the count of three, Wet-Suit and Snake Eyes flung the sharks far away.

"Into the plane!" cried Wet-Suit.
The G.I. JOE teammates slipped inside
through an airtight hatch.
Snake Eyes flipped a switch. The plane
roared to life.

In the cockpit, Wet-Suit crossed two wires. The magnetic field was fixed! *Thunk!* Outside, Storm Shadow and Moray grabbed onto the plane.

"We are taking this plane!" shouted
Storm Shadow. "So watch out!"

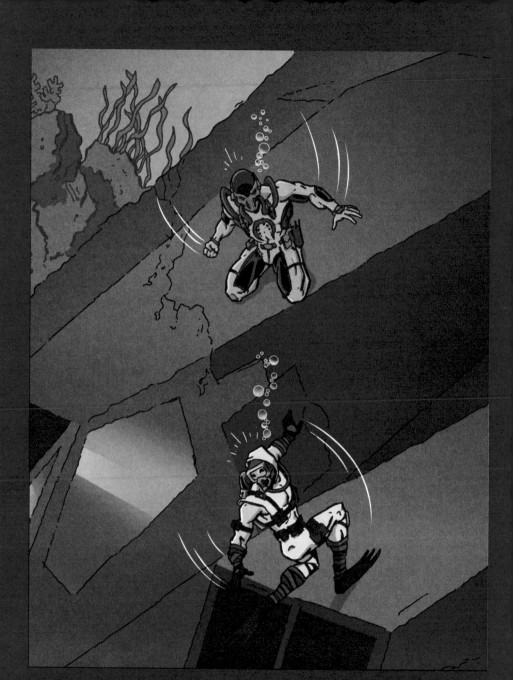

Snake Eyes pressed a button. The plane
seemed to disappear.
But Moray and Storm Shadow still held on
to the invisible walls!

Snake Eyes grabbed a Wind Zapper gun and climbed out to face them.

Snake Eyes aimed — then fired. A powerful blast of air shot the COBRA agents right out of the water!

The stealth plane rose from the waves into the sunshine.

Snake Eyes turned off the device that made the plane invisible.

He and Wet-Suit had done their jobs well today. They had kept the top secret stealth plane out of the wrong hands.

Wet-Suit grinned. "Back to base!" he cheered. "Yo JOE!"